My Cat
Has Kittens

By Gun-Britt Wallqvister
Pictures by Lars Åberg

Harper & Row, Publishers, Inc.

Library of Congress Cataloging in Publication Data
Wallqvister, Gun-Britt, date
   My cat has kittens.

  Translation of: Miss har fått ungar.
  Summary: A young child describes the fun and sur-
prises of a day with her cat Miss's four new-born kit-
tens.
  [1. Cats—Fiction]   I. Åberg, Lars, date, ill.
II. Title
PZ7.W1597Myh   [E]   81-47726
ISBN 0-06-022133-X   AACR2

First American Edition

Miss has four kittens.

When they were just born,
they couldn't see anything.
Their eyes weren't open yet.

They did not know how to walk.
They just stayed in their basket
with Miss.

If Miss left them
for even a little while,
they would cry.

The kittens were hungry
all the time.
Miss fed them milk.

When they were about a week old,
they could open one eye.

When they opened both eyes,
I could tell their eyes were green.

One kitten is black, one is white,
and two have black and white stripes.

Pepper   Salt

Pepper-and-Salt   Salt-and-Pepper

I have given them names.
They are called Pepper, Salt,
Pepper-and-Salt and Salt-and-Pepper.

It is hard to tell which is
Pepper-and-Salt
and which is Salt-and-Pepper.

But if you look closely,
you can see that Pepper-and-Salt
does not have stripes
on one of her ears.
It is all black.

The kittens are full of mischief.
They like to fight.
I tell them to stop
but they don't listen.

They like to play with balls.

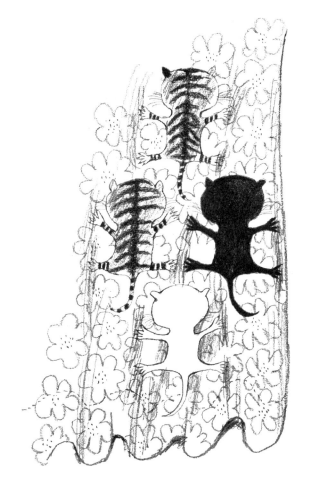

They like to climb on everything.

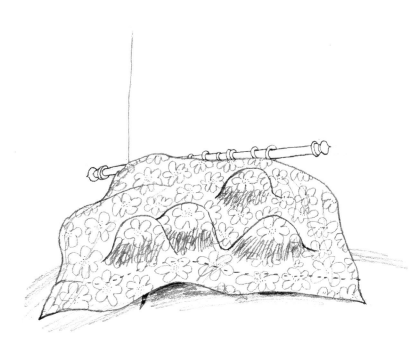

Sometimes that gets them
into trouble.

And they are so nosy!

When they see an open drawer,
they climb in and pull everything out.

If I scold them, they are sorry
and run away to hide.

But when I call them
they come right back.

The kittens are getting bigger.
They drink milk
from their own bowls now.

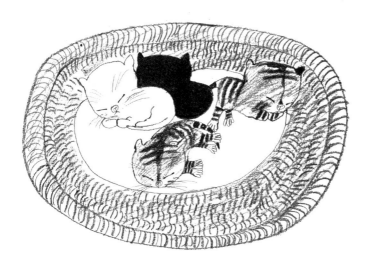

When Miss leaves them for a while
they don't cry anymore.
And when they are tired
they take a nap in their basket.
Shhh!